MRS HONEY'S GLASSES

written and illustrated
by Pam Adams

Child's Play (International) Ltd
Swindon   New York   Bologna
© 1992 Pam Adams   ISBN 0-85953-757-9 (hard cover)   Printed in Singapore
ISBN 0-85953-758-7 (soft cover)

Emma and Peter were staying
with their grandmother,
Mrs Honey.

One morning,
she received a letter.

"Oh, dear!" said Mrs Honey.
"Has anyone seen my glasses?
I can't read this letter
without them."

"Don't worry, Granny,"
said the children.
"We'll help you to look for them."

"I'm going to look
in the chimney," said Peter.

He found some old birds' nests
and got covered in soot.

"You are all black!"
said Emma.

But he didn't find the glasses.

"I'm going to look
in the flour bin," said Emma.

She found a wooden spoon
and a ring
and got covered in flour.

"You are all white!"
said Peter.

But she didn't find the glasses.

"Perhaps I threw them away
by mistake," said Mrs Honey.

She found a bottle
with runny, red sauce in it.

And she found a mouse.
"Eek!" screamed Mrs Honey.

She spilled runny, red sauce
all over her.

"You are all red, Granny!"
laughed the children.

But she didn't find her glasses.

"Maybe, they are in the settee," thought Emma.

Under the cat's cushion, she found a peppermint and a pencil.

Emma was covered in cat's hairs.

"You're all hairy!" scoffed Peter.

But she didn't find the glasses.

"They could be on the top shelf of the kitchen dresser," mused Mrs Honey.

She found some knitting, a string of blue beads, some old photographs, a key and some buttons.

She knocked a box of eggs on the floor.

She was covered in egg.

"You are all yellow!" laughed the children.

But she didn't find her glasses.

"Let's look in the garden,"
said Mrs Honey.

Peter climbed the apple tree.
He found a squirrel
and ate an apple.

"Uggh! It's sour!"
said Peter.

He was green all over.

But he didn't find the glasses.

Emma looked
in the wheelbarrow.

"I've found a caterpillar,"
she said.

She found a gardening glove,
lots of weeds
and grass cuttings.

And she got very green, too.

But she didn't find the glasses.

Peter looked
in the garden shed.

"I've found two super spiders!"
he called.

He found a can of old paint
and he got very blue.

But he didn't find the glasses.

"Maybe, they are in the pond," said Mrs Honey.

She and Emma and Peter looked in the pond.

They found four goldfish and a ball, and they all got covered in slimy, brown mud.

But they didn't find the glasses.

"Goodness!"
exclaimed Mrs Honey.
"Just look at you!
Whatever would
your mother say,
if she saw you like that?

"Let's go indoors
and have a nice, warm bath.
Then I'll put all our clothes
in the washing machine."

But they hadn't found the glasses.

The children had a bath
and brought their dirty clothes
to be washed.

Mrs Honey opened the door
of the washing machine.

"Why, here's my old apron!"
she exclaimed.
"And there is something
in the pocket."

..............................?

"What is it, Granny?"
asked the children.
"We never thought of looking
in the washing machine."

"Hurrah!" cried Mrs Honey.
"I've found my glasses!"

And Mrs Honey put them on.

"Now I can read my letter,"
said Mrs Honey,
after she had put the clothes
in the washing machine.

"Oh, it's from your mother.
She and your father
are coming at five o'clock
to take you to the fair.

"I hope your clothes
will be dry in time."

At five o'clock,
there was a knock at the door.

"Are you ready, children?"
asked Peter and Emma's mother.
"You look as though you have
been sitting very still all day!"

"We've had a lovely time!"
cried Emma and Peter.
"Granny, will you come with us?"

"Of, course," said Mrs Honey.

"Now, where did I put
those glasses?"